WARRIOR'S LAST GIFT

A SHORT STORY

MELISSA MAYHUE

Published by Melissa Mayhue
Copyright © 2012 Melissa Mayhue
Last Updated - 07/2019
Cover art by Inspire Creative Services
All rights reserved.

Print Edition ISBNs:
ISBN-10:0-9908576-3-8
ISBN-13:978-09908576-3-1

Ebook Edition ISBNs:
ISBN-10:0-9908576-2-X
ISBN-13:978-0-9908576-2-4

BOOK BLURB

Life has been hard on Jeanne Harvesson. First she lost the only man she'd ever loved and then she lost her husband, the man who'd been kinder to her than any other. Now, to fulfill his last wish, she risks losing the only thing she has left -- her pride.

Eric MacNicol sacrificed his chance for happiness with the woman he loved, only to watch her wed another as if he'd meant nothing to her. Now he's forced to escort her on a dangerous quest that only proves how little she ever cared for him.

Two stubborn, star-crossed lovers face the journey of a lifetime, but will they return unchanged by the experience or will they discover the true magic of a gift of love?

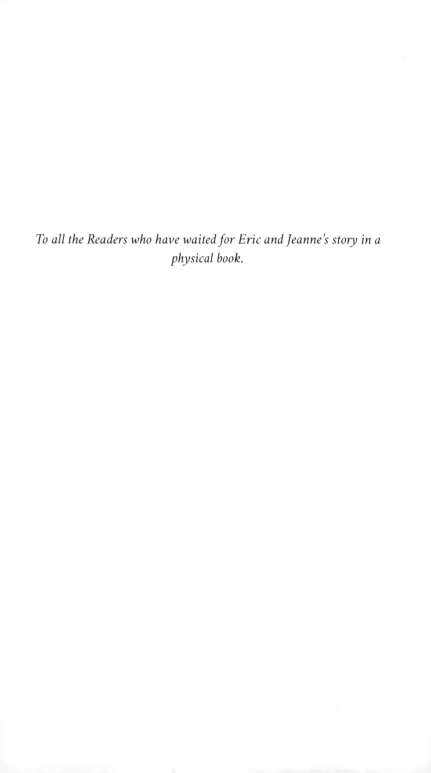

To all the Readers who have waited for Eric and Jeanne's story in a physical book.

PROLOGUE

Castle MacGahan, Scotland
Autumn 1293

*J*eanne MacGhie looked gratefully at the warrior standing in front of her. "I accept yer proposal, Eymer Horvesson. I only pray you ken what it is yer getting yerself into."

"Good. Then I suppose there's no reason for delay." Eymer nervously clasped his hands together behind him.

"None," Jeanne answered, meeting his serious gaze. "None at all."

Eymer had good reason to be nervous. It was a huge step he contemplated.

"Yer sure you want to go through with this?" She had to ask him one last time.

"I am." His head bobbed up and down to reinforce his words. "After what I've confided to you, surely you must ken it's to my benefit as much as to yers. If, that is, yer sure you'll no' regret keeping the truth from Captain MacNicol."

She was more sure of that than of anything else in her life. Though she loved Eric MacNicol deeply, he'd made it more than clear he had no place in his life for a wife and family. His devotion lay entirely in service to their laird.

"I am sure."

She'd never been one to dally over her decisions. There were those who accused her of being rash, but she knew better. If something needed doing, the best course was simply to do it and get it over with. Even something that stole any chance of seeing her dreams come to life.

"It's only that he might have spoken differently if you'd but told him of yer . . ." Eymer paused, a dull red coloring his neck and blotching his cheeks. "Yer condition."

"No."

In this she would not compromise. Jeanne had confessed her love for Eric this very morning, along with her desire to wed as soon as possible. Eric, it seemed, had other priorities in his life. Priorities he'd made abundantly clear in his crisp rejection of her suggestion.

"No," she repeated. "I'd no try to force Eric from his honest desires."

She'd seen the results of such a marriage between her own mother and father.

Eymer, having overheard the whole scene between her and Eric, had followed her when she'd sought privacy beyond the castle walls.

The very idea that someone had heard Eric's rejection of a life with her was beyond humiliating, but there was no time now for self-pity. She had work to do and plans to make. Plans for a future that would not include Eric MacNicol, captain of the guard. Again the pain bit into her heart, forcing her to close her eyes against it. When she opened them again, she found herself staring into Eymer's concerned face.

"That being the case, I'll speak to our laird this very day to see to the arrangements," he said. "We should go back now. We've both much to do in preparation."

Jeanne followed along, feeling the sting of rejection when he fastened his hands behind his back as if to avoid any physical contact with her. She still wasn't sure she believed all he'd told her, but it didn't really matter. If he had spoken the truth, their actions this day would benefit them both.

For her part, she would put away her feelings. Seal them in the deepest, darkest corner of her heart behind a wall of solid stone. It was the least she could do to repay the debt of kindness she would always owe this man. She should consider herself a fortunate woman. Eymer Horvesson was a good man. He'd make a good husband.

Even more important to her right now, he'd make a good father.

CHAPTER 1

Castle MacGahan, Scotland
Winter, 1294

C hewing her own foot off would be more pleasant than what she was preparing to do.

Jeanne MacGhie Horvesson lifted her chin and knocked upon the big wooden door leading to the soldiers' barracks.

"Do I look to be a damned kitchen maid that I might wait upon yer every need? Can you no' open the damned door for yer ownself, you lowlife— Oh." The face of the big man who opened the door to her knock colored a dull red. "Begging yer pardon, Mistress Horvesson. I thought it one of the men who— How may I be of service to you?"

Jeanne wasn't surprised by his reaction. Since Eymer's death in service to their laird, all the men treated her with the utmost respect. Respect she hardly deserved but was determined to earn.

"I wish to speak to yer captain."

In truth, the captain was the last man she wished to speak with, but there was no one else for her to turn to. And she'd given her oath that she would do this.

"If you'll but wait here, I'll see if he's yet returned from—"

"I'm here." Eric MacNicol stepped from the shadows of the long hallway, his gaze riveted on her.

For an instant, it felt as though her foolish body had forgotten how to take its next breath. But then she remembered and forced herself to push aside the anxiety, shoving it back into the secret box where it dwelt. This wasn't about her. She was here for Eymer.

The big guardsman dipped his head respectfully and made a discreet exit as Eric approached her.

"It's well past time that I should have delivered my condolences on the loss of yer . . ." Eric paused, glancing down to his hands and back up again. "On Eymer's death. He was a true warrior and a good man."

"That he was," she agreed. Perhaps the kindest, most caring man she'd ever known.

"Why have you come here? What would you have of me, Je—" He bit her name off, clamping his lips into a thin, straight line before he recovered himself and continued. "Mistress Horvesson."

Jeanne hated the cold blanket of formality and disdain that lay between them, but it was for the best. Besides, she had no more control over Eric's feelings than she did over her own. Were that the case, the last year and half of her life likely would have been a very different story.

She drew a deep breath, once again reminding herself that her visit here today was not about her feelings. Or Eric's. She had a promise to keep.

"I've come to ask a boon of you, Eric MacNicol. A final boon on behalf of Eymer Horvesson."

Eric's expression blanked as if a curtain had dropped

across his eyes, hiding any true emotion. "Tell me what it is you'd have of me. I'll do whatever I can."

"Eymer's wish, his one and only request of me ever, was that should he die, he wanted to receive a proper Viking burial. He wanted his body set adrift in a burning vessel dedicated to the patron god of his family, Thor."

For just an instant, pity shone starkly in Eric's face. "You ken there's naught I can do to make that happen for him, Jeanne. His body canna be reclaimed from the MacDowylt stronghold. His fate would await any who approached Tordenet's gates."

Did he honestly think her that stupid? She knew the laird who'd ordered her husband's death would never release his body to them. But Eymer had considered such a possibility before he'd left Castle MacGahan on his trek north.

"Eymer fully accepted that his death could well come at a time and a place that would deny him that which he wanted most. He planned ahead for such an eventuality." She reached into her pocket and pulled out a small cloth bag, holding it out in front of her, like an offering in the palm of her hand. "Which is why he left this."

Eric took a step back from her, holding up his hands as if to keep her away from him.

"You canna think to influence the Beast of Tordenet with a treasure. He's more silver than he needs now."

Eric must truly think her stupid.

"It's no' a treasure for the MacDowylt I hold in my hand, but a piece of Eymer himself." She opened the bag and slid the contents out onto her palm. "A tooth. His tooth. I gave my vow that should anything happen to him, I'd see this bit of him delivered to the sea north of Skye, where his spirit might have a clear path back to the home of his ancestors."

Eric's jaw clenched in the manner she remembered all too well as he stared at the palm of her hand.

"We canna spare soldiers to traipse off on such a frivolous mission. There's a war in the offing and we've hardly the men we need to protect the castle as it is."

"It's no men I'm asking for, Captain MacNicol." She spit the title at him, hoping to remind him of his duty to his men. The dead as well as the living. "It's yerself Eymer entrusted with this task. You to accompany me to see it done."

Eric blinked. Once, twice, a third time, in rapid succession, as if she'd spoken a language his mind could not comprehend.

"You've gone daft, woman." His hushed voice barely carried to where she stood. "That's a trip of three to four days, easy, and that with good men riding hard, especially this time of year. You'd no' last a full day in the saddle. Yer no' strong enough for the hardships of such a journey."

"I'm stronger than you credit me, Captain." It took strength beyond any he could imagine to endure the heart-pain she'd suffered through and still manage to stand before him now.

He made no attempt to hide his look of skepticism.

"What you propose is no' a leisurely summer ride down to the loch for a day of pleasure."

The shock of a shared memory tingled through her body and she steeled herself against the emotion it carried. Had he chosen a scene from their past to taunt her?

"I never supposed it would be."

"No." He crossed his arms over the broad chest she'd once dreamed of spending the rest of her days nestled against. "No. What you request is no' possible. I'll no' be a party to it."

"I suspected that would be yer response. I warned Eymer as much and bade him choose another. You are no' the man to turn to in a time of need. No' the one to depend upon." She knew that better than anyone. With a withering look, she turned her back on him. "Doona you bother yerself over failing yer man, Eric MacNicol. I'll see it done myownself, I will."

Before she managed two steps, his fingers clamped onto her upper arm, twirling her around to face him. His eyes glowed with an uncharacteristic anger.

"You've no call to say that of me, Jeanne. No call to think it. It's no' me who up and—" He caught himself mid-sentence, once again hiding every scrap of emotion before he spoke again. "You'll do no such thing."

She jerked her arm from his grasp, backing away. "I will do what I've sworn to do. I owe it to Eymer for all he sacrificed for me. I'll seek an audience with our laird. I'll go to Lady Danielle and beg her assistance. One way or another, I will see this done."

Eric clasped his hands behind his back. "They'll no more allow such a foolish errand than I would."

"It makes no difference. If I have to sneak out in the dead of night and find my own way there afoot, so be it. I gave Eymer my oath to see his last wish carried out, and that's exactly what I intend to do. With or without yer help."

* * *

ERIC STARED after the retreating backside of the most determined, deceitful woman he'd ever met. Her visit had done nothing to resolve the question that had plagued him for the past year and a half. How could she pledge her love to him in one breath and then, within days, wed another? If it had been Eymer all along who'd held her heart, what did that say about what had passed between the two of them?

And yet, no woman—at least no woman he'd ever known —would willingly risk her life as Jeanne proposed doing for any man unless she truly loved him. And if she'd truly loved

Eymer, that could only mean that she'd never loved him, in spite of her pretty words.

He huffed out his breath on a sigh and turned away from the sight of her. Jeanne was a part of his life he'd vowed to put away from him. The last thing he needed as he faced the coming war was a conniving woman filling his thoughts.

But that was exactly what confronted him now, leaving him no more choice in this matter than he had in any other.

Her visit forced him to action, though all he really wanted after two straight days in the saddle was to sleep. That wasn't to be. First, he'd need to hunt down Malcolm's brother. Patrick MacDowylt would understand and help him present his case to their laird before Jeanne had a chance to confront him. Once their laird had refused her request, Patrick would be the best to help him make the arrangements necessary to keep the stubborn woman alive.

Heading toward the keep, Eric rolled his shoulders, preparing himself for what was to come. Though he fully anticipated support from Patrick, and their laird himself, it was Jeanne's threat to go to the lady of Castle MacGahan that concerned him. With Lady Danielle on Jeanne's side, his argument, no matter how sensible, could well be to no avail.

Even without their lady's backing, Eric had not one single doubt that Jeanne would do exactly as she'd threatened, setting off on this wickedly foolish quest all by herself no matter who might try to stop her.

She was without question the most impulsive, stubborn woman he'd ever known.

Unfortunately, she also had the distinction of being the only one he'd ever risked losing his heart to. And because of that, if nothing else, he was determined to do everything in his power to keep her safely here within the walls of Castle MacGahan.

CHAPTER 2

"*I*f I'm to help you, Jeanne, first you'll have to help me understand why this is important enough for you to risk your life over."

The lady of Castle MacGahan reached out to cover Jeanne's hand with her own.

"I owe this to Eymer. He stepped in for me when I needed someone to be there. I canna fail him in the only thing he ever asked of me."

Danielle squeezed her hand. "I know you loved your husband, Jeanne. Believe me, I would do anything in my power to change what happened to Eymer. But going off on some quest to the sea, especially this time of year, just because you promised him you would, hardly seems a rational thing to do. I can see why Captain MacNicol refused you. I'm sure Malcolm will, too— unless you can give me some extraordinarily good reason why you should do this."

Jeanne had never intended to share her secrets with another living soul. She'd sworn as much on her honor.

But honor wasn't going to get her what she needed. Her only hope was plain and simple honesty.

11

"I dinna love Eymer in the way you think. No' as a husband, at any rate. Eymer wed me to save me the shame I'd bear when people learned I was with child. He offered himself as husband and father when the babe's real father refused."

Lady Dani's eyes narrowed as she leaned closer. "You meant to tell me there's some selfish bastard waltzing around this castle who got you pregnant and then refused to marry you when he found out about it? That just makes my blood boil."

"Oh no, it's no' at all like that. Eri—" Jeanne caught herself and started again. "The real father never knew I carried his child. I refused to tell him. He is a good and loyal man."

"But you said…" Lady Dani's words trailed off, her expression clearly confused.

"I said he refused to marry *me*. If he dinna want a life with me, I'd no wish to complicate the issue with a child. I was such a child, and the resentment that filled my home was not what I wanted for a babe of my own. Eymer agreed. Eventually."

Though he had nagged her about it for months before… before it was no longer an issue.

Looking away from her companion, Jeanne willed herself not to delve into those still-raw memories.

"So, if I'm hearing you correctly, Eymer wanted the real father to know the truth. Didn't he think that would be a problem down the line when the two of you had children of your own?"

Jeanne took a deep breath, readying herself to reveal yet another secret she'd thought never to share.

"Eymer and I would never have children of our own. From the beginning, he had confided that he was not inter-ested in the charms I had to offer. In truth, he had no interest in the charms any woman had to offer."

Though she had been slow to believe him on that count. Out of a sense of duty as the man's wife, she had tried. But Eymer's honesty had matched his kindness. Women did not appeal to him and soon she had realized the truth in his claim that her child would be his only chance at keeping the Horvesson name alive.

"Well then. Where is this child now?"

The unexpected question pierced Jeanne's heart like an arrow, drawing tears she couldn't hide. "The babe was born too early. He dinna survive."

"Oh, Jeanne." Lady Dani's eyes filled with tears as she leaned close to clasp her arms around Jeanne. "I'm so sorry. I had no idea."

"Few did, my lady." It had been best that way.

They held the embrace for several minutes before Lady Dani sat back in her seat and cast a watery smile at Jeanne as she wiped her hands down her cheeks.

"Very well," she murmured. "You said that in his last request, Eymer specifically insisted that Captain MacNicol accompany you to send him off to his afterlife?"

Jeanne nodded. In spite of all her protests, in spite of her arguments that fulfilling such a vow with Eric MacNicol at her side would be sheer hell for her, Eymer would not be swayed on that point.

Lady Dani asked, "Did you love that man, the father of your child? I must have your complete honesty in this, Jeanne."

"With all my heart," Jeanne answered determined to give her lady the honesty she deserved.

"And Eymer knew how you felt about that man?"

"Aye. But I made it clear that part of my life was behind me."

"I see." Lady Dani nodded once more. "Would I be correct

in guessing that Eric MacNicol is the man we're talking about?"

Jeanne swept her gaze to the floor, hoping the flush heating her cheeks wouldn't give her away.

"It's all right, Jeanne. You don't have to answer that one."

"Will you help me?"

Lady Danielle was her last hope.

"Yes. I'll make sure Malcolm sees the importance of your keeping your oath to Eymer."

"Oh, thank you, Lady Dani. I can never repay this gift."

Lady Danielle smiled, putting her arm around Jeanne's shoulders to give her a hug as they stood and strolled out the door of her solar and into the hall.

"There's nothing to repay, my friend. In fact, I'd suggest it's not me that's giving you a gift, but Eymer."

Eymer? His gift had been giving up his freedom to marry her and be father to her child. The time she would be forced to spend with Eric MacNicol would be no gift. It would be a punishment for all her sins.

CHAPTER 3

*E*ric stretched his back and glanced over his shoulder. If anyone had asked him this time yesterday where he'd be right now, he would have sworn he'd be tucked in his bed, recovering from his recent travels. He certainly wouldn't have guessed he'd be a full day's journey away from Castle MacGahan, headed toward the sea with Jeanne in tow.

And yet here he was, tasked with the responsibility of keeping safe the woman he'd never intended to even speak to again.

"Are you ready for a rest?"

Jeanne shook her head, surprising him once again. He'd pushed her hard from the moment they'd passed through the castle gates, giving her no consideration or leeway. Intentionally, their pace had been more difficult than what he would have set for his most seasoned warriors. His hope had been that she'd give up before the sun set on their first day.

She hadn't. And though her face was drawn with weariness, she continued on even now.

Perhaps he'd underestimated her determination.

He shrugged and turned his back on her, pressing forward.

It wasn't his place to question her decision. No more than it had been his place to question Malcolm when his laird had knocked on his door late last night with orders to act as Jeanne's guardian on her journey to fulfill her husband's last wish. Eric was sure that Jeanne's visit to Lady Danielle was behind the laird's change of heart.

The trees in front of him faded nto one another, much less real to him than his last vision of the woman behind him, struggling to sit up straight in her saddle. She clearly needed rest, whether or not she'd admit to it.

Still, it was she who'd refused his offer, plain and simple. She'd wanted this and now she had it. Her fault and none of his own. Nothing more than what a woman such as she deserved. She'd gotten exactly what she'd asked for.

No matter how he attempted to justify his actions, guilt ate away at his peace of mind liek a rat loosed in the grain stores. He wanted to force her into turning back, not to kill her.

"Bollocks," he muttered under his breath pulling his horse to a halt and turning in his saddle to observe her.

She'd dropped even farther behind that she'd been a few minutes earlier.

"Yer animal looks to be worn down from our day's travel, even if yer no'. If we cut back through the trees here, we're close to a spot that will serve us well this night. He'd camped there often enough with his men to know.

"If you think it best," she responded, her voice barely loud enough to cover the distance between them. "But I'd no have us wasting away our daylight on my account."

"There's no much light left. By the time we see to the horses and set a fire, the sun will have deserted us."

He'd almost have sworn an expression of relief skittered

across her face. Perhaps after a cold night under the stars she'd be more reasonable about returning to the castle. He could hop, though he was beginning to suspect he'd been wrong in his judgment of Jeanne. At least in this one thing.

* * *

THANK ALL THAT WAS HOLY!

Ahead of her, Eric dismounted and led his animal to the stream running alongside the small glen.

She should no doubt do the same. She would, too. Just as soon as she could get her muscles to cooperate enough to allow her to lift her leg over the saddle.

If they ever worked again, that is. Her legs trembled with exhaustion and, Lord, she hurt everywhere.

With Eric's emotionless stare fixed upon her, she forced herself to dismount. She would not give him the satisfaction of thinking he'd been right about her inability to make this journey.

The best she could manage was to pull her leg over the horse's rump so that she rolled to her stomach, intending to slide down the animal's side.

It would have worked, too, had her legs not refused to hold her weight. She felt her toes touch solid earth, but her legs were as weak as bread soaked in milk, collapsing beneath her.

She braced for an impact with the ground, which never came. Instead, Eric's strong arms fastened around her just in time.

"As I thought," he murmured, leaning down to sweep an arm under her legs and carry her to the spot where he'd already deposited his bedroll.

Had she been able, she might have refused his help. She might have held her head high, pushing away from him. She might have insisted that he remove his hands from her at once.

Instead, she allowed herself the luxury of laying her cheek against his broad chest. It had been so long since she'd last taken shelter there.

He dropped to one knee and gently placed her o the ground. "Sit," he ordered before rising to turn his back on her.

It had been a moment of weakness and nothing more. She would give herself that one time considering the hardship of the day.

Eric dropped her things on the ground beside her before leading her mount to drink. Pushing herself up to her knees, she grasped onto the boulder behind her to stand. After a moment to assure herself she wouldn't again topple over, she began, slowly, to gather bits of kindling for their fire.

"I thought I told you to sit. I have this well in hand."

Eric stood across the open ground, his arms crossed over his chest as the last rays of sunlight glimmered through the canopy of trees to form a glow behind him.

She turned her back on him and bent to her work. She'd fallen victim to his charms before, but not this time. This time would be different. It had to be.

"I've no wish to be a burden to you," she managed to croak out around the emotion thickening her throat.

"A little late for that, I'd say."

"I beg yer pardon?" She straightened and tossed her kindling into the ring of stones Eric had already arranged. "I've done nothing to slow you down this day."

"True." He dumped the load of wood he'd gathered on top of hers. "But I'd no be wasting my time upon this journey in the first place if no for you."

"Then go back." Warming to the argument, she pointed in the direction she thought would carry him back to the trail.

If only she could work up a really good anger, dealing with Eric would be so much easier. "Leave now. I've no need for you or yer bad attitude."

He shook his head, his own anger showing through the cracks in his mask. "As if Laird Malcolm would allow such, after yer whining plea for help to his good lady." He cast a scathing glare her direction before turning his attention back to his work on setting the fire. "What pretty words did you say to convince her you should be allowed to risk yer life just to toss a dead man's tooth into the sea?"

How could she ever have imagined herself in love with such a thoughtless brute?

"The Truth. I shared with our lady the truth of why I must keep my oath to Eymer." The whole sordid, painful, embarrassing truth. They'd had a good cry together over it, and then Lady Danielle had promised her everything would work out just fine.

"And what might that truth be?"

"None of yer business, Captain." Her heart pounded in her chest, the need to feign anger no longer necessary. "And as to tossing Eymer's tooth into the sea, I expected better of you than that. After the years you claim to have spent at our laird's home in the north, you of all people should well ken that I've no intention of simply tossing anything into the sea."

Eric didn't look up to meet her eyes, but the muscle in his jaw tightened in a way she recognized all too well.

She wasn't the only one who was angry.

With that knowledge, her own anger fled, leaving her once again defenseless.

"Let me show you," she offered, going to her pack and unrolling it.

She spread the clothing and blankets until she found the treasure she sought, the small wooden boat Eymer had carved, specifically to serve the purpose of being his funeral pyre.

"Here." She held out the boat for Eric to inspect. "Eymer made it himself. Once I've asked Thor's blessing as he instructed, I'll light fire to it and set it on its course into the sea, bearing all that is left of Eymer toward the home of his ancestors."

Eric accepted the vessel from her, holding it carefully in the cradle of his two hands. "The pillow?" he asked, his voice barely more than a whisper.

"Eymer bade me stitch it with our laird's symbol upon it. It's filled with dried herbs to aid in the burning."

Eric handed it to her and turned back to building the fire.

"It willna work, he said at last. "'Tis but a bairn's toy, too small to prevent the first wave from driving it to shore or swamping it."

"Mayhap." She'd worried over that eventuality herself. "But I gave Eymer my oath to see it done, and I've no intention of letting him down."

* * *

HOW HE'D MANAGED to organize their provisions, feed them a meal, and get them both to their rest this night was beyond Eric. Though, as much as he needed it, sleep would be eluding him for quite some time. All he could see when he closed his eyes was the delicate linen pillow Jeanne had sewn, her careful, tiny stitches forming the MacDowylt mark so finely that they might have been drawn on by a monk's trained hand.

The care required, the painstaking detail, the time involved, all pointed to one unmistakable conclusion.

"You loved Eymer."

Cloaked in the dark of night, with the low glimmer of

their banked fire pit their only light, Eric at last voiced the thought that had eaten at his mind for over a year.

He had loved Jeanne, but she had loved another.

The delay between his comment and her reply stretched out until he began to believe she'd not heard him. Perhaps she slept. Or perhaps it was only the layers of blankets and fur wrapped around her for warmth that prevented her from hearing.

She finally said, "Eymer was a good man. Well deserving of love."

Unlike him? She hadn't said those exact words, but he felt the sting as if she had. He had no doubt a declaration of love came easily to her lips. After all, she'd claimed her devotion to him only days before she'd wed Eymer.

But this was different. Eymer was gone and she had no need to impress him any longer and yet, here she was, risking her life to fulfill his final wish. That spoke of real love to him epitomized by the little herb-filled pillow she'd so carefully stitched.

Eric rolled to his side, gazing across the fire's embers to where Jeanne lay, an unmoving bundle of woolens and fur.

No, there would be little in the way of sleep for him this night. The strange pressure in his chest and throat would see to that.

CHAPTER 4

ork through it, Jeanne's mother had always told her. And so she would, even it it meant rising after only a few hours.

Not that she had slept well. Not with *him* lying only a few feet away from her.

She hoisted the heavy kettle of water over the fire and straightened, one hand to her aching back. Her legs trembled with the exertion but she was determined to keep moving. Work would keep her mind busy, and a busy mind was the only way to keep *him* out of her thoughts.

As if it were beyond her ability to control, she glanced to where Eric slept. Apparently he'd tired himself out in yesterday's arduous trek, which, she had no doubt, he'd hoped would convince her to turn back.

She smiled to herself and duped oats into the bubbling water, letting the aroma bathe her face with its steamy goodness.

Eric had seriously underestimated her. Nothing would prevent her setting that little boat out to sea. After all she'd been through in the past year and a half, she'd grown strong enough to face any hardship.

She dropped a handful of dried herbs and berries into the pot and stirred, her gaze drawn once again to the other side of the fire. Even still, the sight of Eric lying there tugged at her heart and stoked a fire low in her belly.

It was more than just how strong and handsome he was. It was the memory of his former kindness, his tenderness, the feel of his hands on her bare skin...

"Oh, pardie!" she whispered, turning her full attention back to the bubbling pot.

She could not do this to herself.

Eric was also stubborn to a fault, and so dedicated to his work that nothing and no one—certainly not she!—could ever compete with his service to his laird.

Again she dipped her head over the pot, breathing in the aromatic steam, forcing away the tormenting thoughts of what might have been.

* * *

THE SAVORY AROMA of porridge awoke him. Eric stretched under the weight of the woolens nd furs that covered him and turned on his side to watch Jeanne bustling around the fire pit.

That she'd managed to get the fire going and cooking started without waking him was proof of his inability to get a decent rest last night, in spite of his exhaustion. He could thank her for that.

She leaned over the pot she stirred, inhaling the steam as it wafted up to bathe her face, heating her cheeks with a rosy glow.

He remembered another time he'd watched her do the same thing. His memory transported him from a cod winter's morn to a warm summer's eve. He had been responsible for the glow in her cheeks that evening. She'd cooked for him, wearing nothing but a flimsy shift that had later fallen from her shoulders at the urging of his eager fingers.

Those fingers trembled now as he scrubbed them over his face. He would not go there again. He couldn't allow his mind to wander down such a painful path.

"You should have wakened me," he growled, throwing back his covers.

Jeanne gasped and dropped her spurtle into the pot, as if she'd completely forgotten she wasn't alone.

"Oh, bother," she muttered, plunging her fingers into the pot to retrieve the utensil and hissing as the hot porridge enveloped her skin.

"By all that's holy!" Eric was on his feet and at her side in an instant. "What were you thinking, woman? You've burned yerself for sure."

"It's nothing," she muttered, lifting the injured fingers to her lips.

Grabbing her around the waist, he hoisted her from her feet and carried her the short distance to the stream, forcing her hand into the icy water despite her protests.

As he held her close, the dizzying scent of herbs filled his nose, and memories washed over him. How often had he wrapped his arms around her, pressing her body to his? So many times, yet not nearly enough.

Their eyes locked and her lips parted in a breathy little sound, as her tongue darted nervously over her soft, full lips.

"My porridge will burn," she whispered, breaking the spell he felt had taken him.

"Better yer porridge than er flesh," he managed, releasing his hold on her.

She hurried away from him and he leaned down, lifting the cold water with trembling hands to splash over his face.

Damn him for the fool he was. Even after all she'd done, he wanted her still.

He dragged the edge of his plaid across his eyes and rose to his feet, his feelings pushed back into the depths of his soul, where they belonged.

What had passed between them just now meant nothing. It had been only a momentary weakness, brought on by his exhaustion and having her so close to him. He wouldn't make that mistake again. From now on, he'd keep his hands to himself and the Fates could deal with Jeanne.

'Best you get that food served up so we can be on our way. We've another long day ahead of us. Unless..." He turned to fix her with a stare. "If you'll but admit the folly of yer quest you could be in yer own bed at Castle MacGahan this very night."

The scathing look Jeanne cast his direction was all the answer he needed. Not that he'd truly expected her to change her mind now. Not after the punishment she'd taken without protest yesterday.

Wordlessly, she broke a chunk of bread from the loaf she held and handed it to him before setting the pot of porridge between them.

They ate in silence, giving his mind too much rein to wander through memories of past meals they'd shared. Memories of the banter, the laughter, the love he was so sure he'd seen in her eyes.

"Fool," he muttered under his breath, tossing the remains of his bread into the trees as he stood.

"Pardon?" She looked up, startled, as if her thoughts had been as far away as his.

"We're wasting light," he grumbled, more bothered than he wanted to admit by the memories swarming thickly around his head. Memories he'd thought buried and gone after all this time.

She followed his lead and began clearing the remains of their camp. In a short time, they were packed up and ready to be on their way once again.

Jeanne stood beside her mount, hands clenching her reins, her chin lifted in resolve like a warrior preparing for her first battle.

Eric's resolve to keep his hands to himself melted as if he'd never made the vow and he strode to her side to grasp her waist and lift her to her saddle.

Her breath caught in a little gasp a sound he remembered all too well. A sound that filled his traitorous body with need and wanting.

He jerked his hands away the moment she was in her saddle and returned to his mount.

If he couldn't convince her to abandon her foolish quest, he had no choice but to get her to the sea and back home again on what was shaping up to be the hardest journey of his life.

* * *

JEANNE HAD TRIED to put Eric from her mind. Tried to ignore his presence. But when he touched her, by the saints, it set her heart pounding and her whole body buzzed with a frenzy of excitement.

Staring at his back she lifted a hand to her cheek, hot again with the thought of his hands upon her as she'd mounted her horse, though that had been many hours past. And when he'd carried her to the stream this morning to plunge her burning fingers into the icy waters, it had taken all her strength not to fasten her mouth upon his and claim him for her own.

Only he wasn't her own, a fact he had made abundantly clear to her.

Truly, she suspected she was losing what few wits she had left. To harbor such feeling for the man who's rejected her was the height of foolishness.

And yet, what she wouldn't give to hear him speak her name.

"Stay close and keep a wary eye."

His voice was so low, she thought for a moment she'd imagined him speaking.

"There's someone on the trail, coming toward us."

In almost two full days of travel, this was the first person they'd seen and, from Eric's tone, it sounded as thought he was none too pleased.

Jeanne craned her neck to see around her companion, spotting the figure ahead, arm raised in greeting.

"He looks to be friendly enough," she offered. "And much smaller than you."

Aye. Mayhap he's also bait to draw us into a trap."

Eric drew up o his horse's reins, dropping back beside her, surprising her when he touched her hand. He surprised her even more when she saw that he held a wicked-looking dagger in the hand that lay over hers.

"Take this." He pulled the hem of her cloak over her hand, concealing the weapon. "Keep it at the ready."

"Surely yer being overly cautious, she scoffed.

"Better overly cautious than overly dead," he responded darkly, returning to his spot ahead of her. "If the need arises, head for the woods. You'll be harder to find there."

Fear knotted in Jeanne's stomach. Not until they drew close enough to see the traveler's face did she relax.

"He's naught but a lad," she said.

"A weapon's no particular about the age of the one who wields it. Stay on yer guard, Jeanne."

Eric could well be right, but the boy looked harmless

enough to her. Harmless and cold dressed in those think clothes, with not even a fur to protect him.

"Aho," the boy called out with a grin as they reached him. "A fair gift it is to see fellow travelers on the road! I'm Dobbie Caskie." The boy lifted a hand in greeting toward Eric.

Eric simply stared at the boy until he let the hand drop back to his side.

"I doona suppose you'd consider sharing yer fire and an extra portion of food this night?" The boy licked his lips his eyes darting from Eric to Jeanne and back again.

"No," Eric answered.

"We most certainly would," Jeanne corrected, ignoring Eric's head snapping around in her direction.

The boy couldn't have been more than twelve or thirteen, and he looked to be freezing out here all by himself. Sharing their fire and food for the evening was the least they could do to help him.

"Thank you, my lady. It's no charity I'm asking. I'm willing to work for it. I can help set up yer camp and gather wood for you. Whatever you need."

"And work for it you will, my young friend," Eric promised, glaring at Jeanne, leaving her no doubt she'd be hearing about this later.

* * *

"It's a mistake we make, taking that one in." Eric glared at her as he took the pail of water from her hand and turned back to their campsite. "I feel it in my bones."

"Yer brainsick," Jeanne replied. And heartless, too, if you think to turn away a slip of a lad who needs our help. Shame on you for letting yer unfounded suspicions rule you."

With a sharp nod of her head, she pushed in front of him

ad hurried back toward the fire, where their young guest was finishing his meal.

"This is so good." Dobbie looked up from his porridge as they neared and he cast a helpful eye toward the pot.

Considering how much of the setup work he'd done when they reached this site, Jeanne felt he'd more than earned his meal.

"There's more. Help yerself, lad." She smiled to encourage him, but clearly, he didn't need her encouragement. The boy acted as if he were half starved.

"What are you doing out here traveling all by yerself? Eric sat apart from them, a frown fixed between his brows. "With no pack and no provisions of yer own?"

"I'm on my way to Skye," the boy answered around a mouthful of bread. "To my mam's folk, the MacCabes. With both my mam and da gone, it seemed the best thing to do. I had food in the beginning, but no enough to last the whole of my trip."

Jeanne's heart went out to the boy. "Then it's good fortune indeed that our paths crossed."

"Aye." Dobbie nodded his head vigorously up and down, his eyes wide. "And thankful I am, too. I've heard tell of thieves who travel these trails. Men who will take yer animals and yer provisions."

"And yer life, if yer no so careful," Eric added.

"Aye." Dobbie nodded in agreement. "A man must be careful about who he chooses to trust when he's out on the road."

To Jeanne's way of thinking, a boy needed to be even more careful. "Yer welcome to accompany us for as long as our paths are the same," Jeanne offered.

"And how would you envision that will work?" Eric's glare turned in her direction again. "We're mounted and he's afoot. He canna run the whole day and we canna afford to slow down to his pace."

She hadn't really thought about it before offering; she only knew that Dobbie needed their help. "The lad can ride upon my horse with me. The extra weight canna make that much of a difference in our progress."

Eric shook his head in clear disgust as he downed the last of his drink. "Best we get some rest then. We'll need an early start if we're to be moving slower on the morrow."

He spread his bedroll and lay down, pulling his woolen up over his head, clearly done with them.

Obstinate, heartless man!

Dobbie finished his food and then assisted Jeanne in packing their belongings in preparation to turn in tor the night. He was so eager to be helpful, she hadn't the heart to correct the way he'd stuffed things into their bags. She could easily sort it all out in the morning when she fixed their next meal.

When they were done, Dobbie lay down next to the embers of their fire with nothing for bedding but the plaid he wore.

"Here," she said, spreading her fur over him. "I've more woolens than I need to keep me warm. You take this."

The boy's grateful smile as he drew the fur tightly around him was all the thanks Jeanne needed to keep her warm. If her son had ended up on his own in the world, she could only pray someone would have shown similar mercies to him.

A familiar pain tightened around her heart as she pulled her covers up to her chin. Her soon, born months too early, would never suffer as this boy did. Her son lay in the arms of the angels and, with the path she'd chosen in life, she wasn't likely to ever have another.

She stared up at the twinkling lights in the dark sky and

knew sleep wouldn't come any easier this night than it had on the last.

* * *

JEANNE AWOKE WITH A START, a sense of dread weighing her down. Likely it was no more than the sorrow on her mind when she'd finally drifted off to sleep or perhaps a bad dream. She pushed up to one elbow and looked across the embers of the fire to see the spot where the boy had slept was empty.

"Dobbie?"

She kept her voice low to avoid waking Eric. Tossing off her covers, she stood and looked around in time to see Dobbie mounted on her horse, the reins To Eric's mount clutched in his free hand.

"It's sorry I am, my lady," he called as he turned the horse around. "Yer a kind soul, but I did warn you to be careful of the company you choose to keep upon the road. Hyah!"

He kicked the horse and bolted forward at a run.

"By the saints!" Eric was on his feet, sword drawn, running across the clearing.

He stopped, pursed his lips, and let out a shrill whistle. His horse reared to its hind legs, jerking the reins from Dobbie's hand to race back to Eric's side.

"I'll remember you, Dobbie Caskie!" Eric shouted at the boy's retreating back. "Best you be looking over yer shoulder!"

It all felt like some horrible nightmare. "I canna believe the lad would—" Jeanne began.

"Believe it," Eric interrupted. "Perhaps in the future, you won't be so critical of my suspicions. Unfounded or otherwise."

Eric turned away from her, leaving her to stare into the darkness that had swallowed any sign of the boy.

"Bollocks," Eric growled from behind her. "The little whoreson has made off with the better share of our provisions."

No wonder he'd stuffed so much of the food into one sack when he'd helped to clean up. He'd already known what he planned to do.

"Well, we've no choice now." Eric stood facing her, hands on his hips. We'll return to Castle MacGahan at first light."

"No, we won't." Not as long as she had breath in her body. "Thanks to yer clever training, we still have yer horse. There's no reason for us to turn back."

"No reason?" Eric's voice rose in pitch. "Who's brainsick now? Do you ken how much longer it will take us? We've no' enough food left to carry us to the coast, let alone home again."

"Go home yerself, then, if you want. I'll walk to the sea if I have to. I swore an oath and I mean to keep it."

The shadows hid Eric's expression, but she had no need to see it. His mumbled swearing told her all she needed to know. He didn't agree with her, but he wouldn't desert her, either.

This might be a setback to their plans, but she wouldn't allow it to prevent her from keeping her promise to Eymer.

CHAPTER 5

*H*eavy clouds blanketed the sky all the way to the horizon as their path ascended up the great mountainside. Jeanne buried her face in the furs covering Eric's back, holding tightly against the winds that buffeted their progress.

Their stops were more frequent today, owing to his horse having to carry the both of them, but she couldn't be upset about that. Not when it meant more time to walk around and stretch her legs. Not when it meant spending her day so close to him.

Early this morning, riding pressed up against him as she was now, she'd given up the last vestiges of hope that she'd ever be able to exorcise him from her heart. And though they'd likely never cross paths again after their quest came to an end, she'd decided to give herself this time of pleasure being close to him. In her imagination, for at least the next several days, he could once again be *her* Eric.

"We'll rest here for a bit," he said over his shoulder. "There's some small shelter from the wind up against the rocks and there's water."

Once Eric had dismounted, he lifted his arms to help her down. "Stay close," he cautioned, leading his horse back down the incline to the water.

Jeanne pulled her woolen tightly around her, sorely missing the fur that Dobbie had taken with him. She placed a hand to her neck and stretched. The bundle of her most precious belongings strapped to her back was responsible for the ache in her shoulders, but a short walk to stretch her limbs would help.

Small patches of snow lay in the shadowed spots and she watched her feet to avoid slipping on them as she made her way up and around the rise toward the peak. Bushes, wild and tangled like a miniature wind-ravaged forest, stood between her and the spot she had her sights set upon. Carefully she made her way through them, stopping a couple of times to free her cloak from the thorny grasp of the undergrowth as she climbed.

Only feet from the edge of the summit, she tightened her cloak against the bitter wind and dropped to her knees to admire the view. Mountain peaks stretched out in the distance, cupping a lake-filled valley below.

When she heard a noise behind her, she assumed Eric had followed.

"Isn't it beautiful?" she asked, turning with a smile to find herself staring into eyes as yellow as a summer sunset.

A wolf!

He'd arrived on silent feet and now he stood unmoving, his eyes fixed on her as if she might be his next meal.

"Eric?" she called, her voice so quiet she knew her companion would never hear. But would the creature pounce if she startled it by yelling? She tried again, a little louder. "Eric?"

Slowly, so as not to frighten the animal, she stood, hunched at first, then straightened to her full height.

The animal didn't move. Jeanne wasn't even sure he'd blinked those piercing yellow eyes

"Eric! She screamed, as the wold lifted a massive paw to move in her direction.

A small figure darted from behind her in a streak of white fur, and, startled, she jerked backward. Her foot slid into a pile of snow sheltered by a low ridge of rock that bit into her calf and tilted her off balance. Her arms flailed uselessly as she fought to catch herself, and with another step back, her foot hit nothing but air, pitching her over the side of the cliff.

* * *

ERIC COULD HAVE SWORN he heard Jeanne call his name, but when he turned, she wasn't in the spot where he'd left her.

"Bollocks," he grumbled. Hadn't he told her to stay close? He had more to do than spend his time trying to hunt her down if she got herself lost up here. Though, with so few trees, getting lost would be a difficult task, even for Jeanne.

"Eric!"

That scream certainly wasn't his imagination. He spun toward the sound, pulling his sword from its scabbard his eye tracking upward.

She stood at the highest point on the promontory, suspended for one brief moment against the stark gray sky, her arms askew above her head before she tumbled over backward, disappearing from sight.

"Jeanne!"

He ran as heard as he could, scrambling up the side of the incline. His stomach knotted so tightly, each breath was a battle.

"Jeanne!"

He paused at the summit only long enough to scan the area and the vast space of nothing on the other side. His heart pounded in his chest as he approached the edge and peered over, fearing he'd find the worst.

Approximately eight feet below him, Jeanne lay on her back on a small jagged outcropping of rock, one leg dangling off the edge to a sheer drop below.

"Jeanne? Can you hear me?"

She groaned and lifted a hand to her head, shifting her position as if she thought to sit up.

"Doona move!" he yelled down to her.

"Is the beast—Holy Mother!" she screamed as she realized where she was.

"Doona you panic!" he ordered. "I'll no' let anything happen to you. You hear me? Just be calm and we'll get you up from there."

"Ha!" she responded, sounding a bit more like herself. "Well, I'm no' climbing up there, I can tell you that."

She was right. Climbing up the sheer drop didn't look to be an option.

"I'll be right back," he called down. "Doona you move."

He turned to race back down to where his horse waited with a coil of rope securing their belongings together.

When he returned, she was sitting with her back pressed up against the face of the cliff, her arms wrapped around the bundle of her possessions she'd carried on her back.

After tying one end of the rope to his horse, he dropped to his knees at the edge of the cliff.

"I'm going to pass a rope down to you, Jeanne. Are you listening to me? I need you to secure it around yerself and knot it tightly under yer arms so I can pull you back up."

He slid the end over the edge, working it down to her. When it reached her, rather than tying it around herself as he'd told her to, she began to tie it to the bundle in her arms.

"What are you doing?"

"Te ties have broken and I canna very well hold the rope to climb if I'm holding this bundle instead, now can I?"

"Leave the damn bundle," he shouted down. "It's you we need to get up, no' that worthless pile of clothing."

"It's no' worthless," she argued, continuing in her task. "I've the dagger you gave me and Eymer's tooth and the vessel he carved! I canna leave them behind."

Eric rubbed a hand over his face, irritation warring with the swell of fear that had engulfed him. Clearly, arguing with her would do him no good. Her stubbornness knew no bounds, not even when her safety was at risk.

"Send it up."

He peered back over the edge to find her working furiously to open the bundle she had just secured.

"What are you doing now?"

She didn't answer, her head bowed to her work.

"Jeanne. You canna spend the whole of the afternoon down there. We need to get moving before we lose the light."

She hesitated for a moment, but nodded her agreement, once again tying the bundle to the rope before holding it up over her head.

Finally.

After the bundle was on the ground beside him, he slid the rope back down to her and waited while she tied it around herself.

"Check the knots again," he instructed. "And hold on as if yer very life depended upon it."

It just might.

With a click of his tongue, his horse began to back away, assisting him in pulling up the rope and its precious cargo. As soon as her hands were within his reach, he grabbed them and hoisted her up until her feet were solidly on the ground next to his.

Her face was streaked with dirt, her cheek scraped and

bloodied, and her hair was brambles clinging to it, but he'd never seen her look more beautiful.

"Thank all that's holy for the ledge below," he whispered as he wrapped his arms around her and crushed here to his chest. He covered her mouth with his, breathing her in as he held her trembling body close. He could have lost her. He'd thought he had.

When he felt strong enough to release her, she stepped back from him, her hands covering her cheeks.

"There was a wolf," she said, looking around the ground at her feet. "And a rabbit. And then I fell ad hit upo my back."

Pain and fear lanced through her expression, but before he could pull her close again, she slumped to the ground at his feet, scooped up her bundle, and began one more to tear into it.

"I ken you've had a fright, Jeanne, but yer find now. The wolf and his prey are long gone. Yer safe and we need to be on the move again. The daylight will be gone quickly enough, and I'd hoped to be in the shelter of trees before we set camp this night."

"It's of no matter," she whimpered, her head bent over the bundle in her lap.

He'd been wrong. She had been hurt. He hadn't even stopped to consider as much when he'd pulled her to safety. All he'd wanted was to held her in his arms to reassure himself that she was alive.

"Where are you hurt? Let me help you."

She turned a tear-streaked face up to him. "You canna help me now. There's no point in going on. Look what I've done. I've ruined it."

In her hands she held the little boat Eymer had carved, broken into two pieces.

"I've failed him," she whimpered, drawing the broken

pieces close to her heart. "The only thing he ever asked of me and I've failed him."

This was the opportunity he'd wanted. With a word, he could easily have them on their way home, this foolish quest no more than a bad memory.

And yet…

He couldn't bear to see her spirit broken like this.

"Doona you fret over it, Jeanne. I can fix it for you. Put it back in yer pack, and when we make camp this night, I'll repair Eymer's boat good as new."

"You think you can?" Se looked yp, such hope and faith shining in her eyes. "You really think you can?"

"I can." He would. Somehow.

All he'd need would be some ashes and some tree sap and time to brew a pitch to seal the boat. No matter that sap ran in the spring, not the winter. If ever the gods of his laird's people were needed, this was that time.

"You hear that, Thor?" he whispered as he turned his back to gather up the rope and repack their things. "It's now or never."

CHAPTER 6

*O*nly a fool would be foraging through trees this time of winter in search of sap. Eric had known he wouldn't find any before he'd left the campsite, but the look of hope in Jeanne's eyes had driven him to make the attempt.

He didn't want to think of her expression when he returned empty-handed, unable to do more than tie the little boat together with strips of cloth.

It shouldn't matter to him in the least. She'd been the one who'd up and married another man. The moment he'd heard, he'd vowed never to spare her another thought. A useless vow if ever he'd heard one. He knew that now.

He was a man who didn't care to deal with his own emotions. He avoided confronting those emotions head-on, preferring to hide within the comforting walls of anger. He would also admit to taking more than a generous time to consider his options when he had a decision to make. These were his faults, and he was all too aware of them.

But standing at the foot of the rise today and watching Jeanne topple off the other side had nearly killed him. Losing her to another man had been bad enough. Truly losing her was something he couldn't bear. Just as he couldn't bear seeing her broken and defeated.

He couldn't fail her in this. He'd promised to fix that damn boat of hers and he would do everything in his power to make it so.

Which was why he was out here, traipsing through the barren wood on a fruitless task to enable her to fulfill a vow based on some ridiculous ancient religion.

Which of them was the more foolish?

"So much for yer Viking belief," he muttered aloud. "So much for Eymer's faith in the great Thor's might power."

He stopped to check his bearing, making sure he hadn't traveled so far from their campsite that he couldn't hear Jeanne if she needed him. Boat or no', he wouldn't risk a chance of having harm come to her because of his carelessness. He'd already managed to lose one of their horses by deferring to her judgment. He wouldn't make a mistake like that again.

A furry figure darted onto the path ahead of him. A large rabbit stared his direction as if it waited for him, making no attempt to conceal its presence.

Fresh meat! Considering the food stores they'd lost to that damned Dobbie Caskie, a rabbit would be a welcome addition to their fare.

Cautiously, slowly, Eric slid his hand to his boot to retrieve the dagger he kept there. Before he could lift his arm, the little beast bounded off the trail into the trees beyond.

Eric followed, his dagger at the ready, led on by the sight of a wisp of fur darting through the underbrush. He broke through into a clearing as the rabbit came to a stop next to a massive evergreen tree. Keeping his gaze fixed on the animal, Eric moved forward only a few steps before his toe caught on a root hidden in the leaves and debris, sending him headfirst toward the tree.

He went down on his knees, landing with a grunt against the tree trunk, barely managing to get his arms out in front of him in time to break his fall.

The dagger he clutched embedded itself into the tree and he used it for leverage to pull himself up to his feet.

What a fool he was! Even the youngest of lads knew well enough to check their footing during a hunt.

With an effort, he pulled his dagger from the tree, amazed to see the blade glistening with moisture. He touched a finger to the metal to find it coated with a tick, sticky substance.

Impossible!

"My apologies for doubting you, Thor," he called out, hurrying to retrieve a cup from his sporran to hold beneath the spot on the tree where sap ran freely. This shouldn't be happening, but it was.

Across the glade, leaves rustled and the rabbit hopped back into sight.

With a flick of his wrist, Eric sent the dagger flying, hoping that Thor was still feeling particularly generous.

* * *

JEANNE POKED at the fire with a stick, sending embers dancing up into the air. The sun had set quite some time before, and soon there would be no light other than this fire to guide Eric back to her

She added another piece of wood and jabbed at the fire again, guilt and misery warring for her complete attention.

It was bad enough that she'd broken the little boat Eymer had so carefully carved. If anything were to happen to Eric, too...

She couldn't allow herself to linger on that path of thought. He was an excellent warrior, quite capable of taking care of himself no matter how far he traveled or how long he stayed away.

Pulling her cloak tighter around her, she winced from her bruises nd scrapes. Every bone in her body hurt, and no doubt she would be even more sore and stiff tomorrow.

She scooted back a little from the blistering heat of the roaring fire and tossed another stick into it.

"How does roasted hare sound for our meal this night?"

Eric stood just inside the circle of their camp, grinning like a fool as he hoisted a huge, skinned animal into the air.

Jeanne had never been so happy to see anyone in tge whole of her life. She was on her feet, racing to him in spite of her injuries. She threw her arms around his neck, almost toppling him over.

"Whoa," he laughed, wrapping his arms, rabbit and all, around her. "You must be hungry indeed, because that's what I calla mighty hearty greeting for a man bearing fresh meat."

"You were gone overlong," she said. "And with the setting of the sun, I feared for yer finding yer way back to me."

His arms tightened around her before he broke the contact. He stepped away quickly, as if he'd remembered the chasm existing between them that, in the moment, she'd clearly forgotten.

"Some fine warrior you must take me for, that you think I'd no' be able to find my way back to this spot," he scoffed. "Besides, you might as well have set a welcome banner to the entire western half of Scotland with the fire you've built. Is there any wood left in the forest?"

Perhaps she had gone a little overboard with the size of the fire, but he was back now, so she'd accomplished what she'd hoped with it. That was what mattered.

Once the rabbit was threaded on a spit and sizzling over

the flames, Jeanne returned to her seat by the fire and turned her attention to the little pot Eric stirred.

"What's that you've got there? It smells awful." Surely he didn't think to add whatever that was to their meal.

"Tree sap and ash, which, thanks to yer zealous efforts, we've plenty of." He looked up with a grin, continuing to stir. "And a few rabbit droppings for strength."

That could certainly account for the smell.

"And you brew that concoction for…?"

He looked up from his work and seemed, for the first time, to understand her suspicions.

"You've no call for concern, sweet Jeanne, I assure you." Merriment danced in his eyes in a way she hadn't seen in far too long. "When this vile mixture is done, I'll use it to repair Eymer's wee vessel, making her seaworthy once again. Now, have we a cloth to tear into strips to hold her together once this is ready?"

She nodded, unable to answer, and turned away to dig through her pack.

Sweet Jeanne.

Hearing the words slip so naturally from Eric's lips stole her breath away and left her feeling weak. Though he didn't even appear to notice he'd used the endearment that had belonged only to him.

She tore strips from the bottom of her spare shift and handed them over to him, watching with interest as he nudged a hot rick from the fire pit and set his pan on it.

"Would it no be faster to hold it over the fire?"

He shook his head, continuing to stir. "That would be a very bad idea. This mixture is too likely to burst into flame. Slow and steady is the only way to prepare it.

All through their meal, Eric fussed with the mixture he brewed, absently picking at the meat she placed beside him, while letting his porridge grow cold. At long last, the contents of the pot me his approval and he spread the goo over the broken edges of the little boat. He then bound the cloth strips around his work to fasten the pieces tightly together.

Do you think that will hold?" Jeanne stared at the mass of bandages. "Do you think it will float?"

Though his meal had grown cold, Eric ate it now like a starving man.

"It will float as well as it would have before the accident," he answered confidently. "What the seas will do to it, I can only guess."

Unexpected tears prickled in Jeanne's eyes and she turned her head, feeling foolish at her unchecked emotion. The day's events had apparently caught up with her.

With a sigh that caught in her throat, she rose to her feet and rolled out her blankets for the night. She climbed into her bedding, wishing she could sleep without worry for just this one night, though she knew it was not to be.

Her body hurt too much for her to find a comfortable position on the hard ground, and her emotions were so raw she felt too vulnerable to sit and talk with Eric without the risk of embarrassing herself with tears.

The fall, the broken boat, her unreasonable fear that Eric would not return, even Eric's gentle kindness—it was all too much for one day.

Perhaps if she could just lie here in the silence, refusing to let herself drift through the memories that always haunted her, she would have a chance to recover herself before morning.

"Jeanne? I'm sorry." Eric's voice drifted softly across the space between them.

"You've no reason to apologize," she called from inside her cocoon of blankets. "You saved my life. And without the work you did this night, I'd no' be able to keep my oath to

Eymer. If anything, it's me that should be apologizing for causing you so much trouble."

"That's no' what I meant." His voice was closer now, as if he'd moved to her side of the fire. "You made it clear to me from the beginning that you wanted a home and a family. I'm sorry Eymer's death robbed you of what you wanted most. I'm sorry about what happened to Eymer. And I'm sorry that I've not been able to say this to you before now. I couldna say these things to you because I… I couldna accept the idea of you married to another man. I thought of you as mine, and yer love for a man other than me was something I could not bear to think upon. It was selfish of me, but there it is."

Jeanne untangled her blankets and sat up, forcing herself to meet Eric's gaze. Raw emotion filled his eyes, and his honesty forced hers.

"I dinna ever love Eymer."

"Then why did you marry him?" he demanded, rising to pace away from her. "After all yer talk of the importance of love, why would you agree to wed? If you dinna love him, why do you risk yer own safety on this foolhardy mission to fulfill his last request?"

"It is the right thing to do," she answered, pulling the blanket back up over her shoulders and lying back down.

She refused to answer any more of his questions, suspecting she had already said more than she should have. That last admission had cost her all she had left to give tonight. Anything more and the flood of memories would leave her a weeping mess. Either that, or she would break down and confess everything.

And neither of those was an outcome she wanted.

CHAPTER 7

When the first raindrops began to pepper down, Eric wasn't surprised. The sky had been heavy and gray when they had awakened, and the temperature had dropped steadily as they traveled. Late in the day, the rain gradually turned to snow.

The heavens themselves seemed determined to keep them from reaching the coast. He'd hoped to make it out of the mountains before they made camp, but that was not to be. At least here there were caves that would provide them shelter from the snow.

"We'll make camp here for the night," he said over his shoulder as he reined his horse to a stop.

He dismounted and held out his arms to assist Jeanne down from the big animal. She fell against him, groaning as her feet hit the ground. Clearly, her tumble over the cliff yesterday had taken its toll.

He swept her from her feet and carried her to the cave's entrance, setting her down inside the opening.

They'd gotten lucky for a change. The cave was just large enough for the two of them, the horse, and a fire. It was crowded, but certainly better than sleeping out in this weather.

Once he had the fire built, Jeanne pushed up from where she sat to gather her pot and what little food they had left.

"You rest," he told her, taking the pot from her hands. "I can do this."

She didn't argue, confirming his suspicion that she was exhausted and in pain.

He filled the pot with snow and set it over the fire to melt. When the water bubbled, he dumped in the last of their oats, along with a few pieces of meat left from last night's rabbit.

"You must remember to stir," Jeanne cautioned without opening her eyes.

As if he weren't perfectly capable of cooking his own food.

When it was ready, he carried the pot over to where she sat, placing it on the ground between them.

"This is the last of our bread," he said, breaking the piece in half to share. "We'll need to keep a sharp eye out for any sign of game tomorrow."

He scooped a bite of the porridge and wrinkled his nose. The tasteless lumps in his mouth had nothing to do with the bits of meat he'd added.

Across from him, Jeanne coughed and grabbed for the flask of ale.

"It seems to lack the flavor of yers," he admitted "And mayhap it has a few more lumps."

"I warned you to stir," she said, keeping her gaze fixed on the food in front of her.

They passed the remainder of their meal in silence, and when they finished, he again filled the pot with snow and set it near the fire. The melt would help to clean the pot in the morning.

By the time he finished, Jeanne had curled into her blankets, her back turned to him.

Though he didn't doubt she was tired, he suspected she wanted to avoid any attempt on his part to push for the answers she'd refused him last night.

Though her comment had eaten away at his thoughts all day, he wouldn't try to force her to answer his questions. It made little difference now anyway. What was done was done. He would simply put it from his mind. There was nothing to be gained from opening old wounds.

And yet...

"Are you awake, Jeanne?"

An audible sigh wafted from the blanket where she huddled. "I am."

"I ken you've no stomach for talk of this, but it preys mightily upon my thoughts. If you dinna love Eymer, why did you take him for yer husband?"

Hadn't she told him that she'd rather spend her days in an empty house than live the lie of a loveless marriage as her mother and father had? And now she'd admitted to marrying a man she hadn't loved. Could it be that he was somehow responsible for what she'd done?

He had to know.

"I need sleep, Eric. I canna speak on this now. I canna even bear to think upon it."

"For a year and a half we've avoided speaking of it. I'd have yer answers now, Jeanne." Eric moved to sit beside her. "The day you wed Eymer Horvesson was the worst of my life. After what we shared, you owe me honesty. At the very least, you owe me an explanation as to why you did it."

"*Owe* you?" Jeanne sat up, tossing blanket aside, her eyes flashing with anger. "I owe you nothing! You claim that as the worst day of yer life? I'm so sorry I forced you into finding *another* foolish maid to take to yer bed. Worst day?

Ha! I could tell you a thing or two about what a worst day truly looks like."

Her anger sparked his, as their emotions had always built upon each other's.

"Truly? I'd imagine a worst day for you might have something to do with falsely proclaiming yer love for one man while planning to wed another. One you now claim you held no love for, even after all yer protestations about how you would never marry for less than love. I can hardly wait to hear what yer idea of a worst day could possibly be."

You want the truth? Then you'll have it." She clenched her fists in her lap and took a deep breath. "It's holding the tiny lifeless body of yer son in yer arms and then watching at the midwife takes him away, leaving you alone with nothing but yer shattered dreams. That's *my* worst day, Eric MacNicol. A day such as I would not wish on my worst enemy.

Eric's stomach lurched as tears filled her eyes and ran down her cheeks. He reached out for her as her body shook with silent sobs, pulling her into his embrace to comfort her.

What a beast he was to push her like that. Only a selfish, heartless fool would treat the woman he loved in such a thoughtless manner.

And love her he must, because only a fool in love would have such a driving need to know what he had done to lose her.

He held her tightly, stroking a hand through her hair and down her back, wishing he ould take away the pain by the strength of his embrace.

It was as if, once her reserve had broken down, she'd lost all control. He had done that to her. He had pierced the armor of her strength and all he felt for having done so was an overwhelming sense of shame.

"Shhh," he consoled as he continued to stroke her hair. "I had no idea you'd been through such heartbreak, Sweet

Jeanne. It's my own selfish pride what lies behind my pushing you for an answer. Just as it was selfish pride that kept me from coming to you after Eymer's death."

"I am all too familiar with the burdens of pride," she managed between hiccuping sobs.

"But mine was beyond the pale. Selfish and foolish. I loved you, and when you chose another over me, I couldna make my peace with what you did. Not until yesterday, when I saw you topple from the mountain crest and I thought I'd lost you all over again. In that moment I realized, pride be damned."

She tipped her head back to look up at him, her breath still catching with emotion.

"I dinna choose another over you, Eric. You rejected me, leaving me no choice at all."

"How can you say you had no choice" He kissed her forehead and her eyes fluttered shut. "I loved you then, Jeanne, and I love you still. There's nothing can do to change the heartbreak you've suffered—the loss of Eymer and his son before him."

"But—"

He silenced her with a kiss, taking her soft lips with his own, turning her words into a quiet moan. Her head dropped back as he inched the kiss from her mouth to her neck, stopping to nibble on her shoulder before he continued to bare his soul.

"I was the one left with no choice. I refused to marry you to save you from this exact sorrow. With war on the horizon, I'd no way to know what would happen. I loved you too much to leave you a grieving widow."

She gasped as he pushed the shift from her shoulders to trail his tongue over her heated skin. The old, familiar need washed over him, hardening his body and driving his actions.

He wanted her. As if the past year and a half had never happened, his need for her was as all-consuming as it had ever been.

He kissed her again, lowering her to her back and taking his place on top of her.

She made no effort to refuse him, but he felt reluctance in her response.

"Did you no' understand that I would have grieved yer loss whether we were married or no'? Though yer intentions were honorable, by yer refusal to take me to wife, you left me in a far worse position that if I had been widowed."

"I canna see how that's possible," he murmured, his mind too occupied with the woman in his arms to concentrate on her words.

"Since you want my honesty, I'll tell you how." Her fingers tightened on his arms, gripping him as a drowning woman might. "It was no' Eymer's son who died in my arms, Eric. It was yers."

* * *

ERIC'S MUSCLES stiffened under her grasp, and the hands that had lovingly stroked her only seconds before now deserted her as he pulled away.

"*My* son?" He shook his head as if to deny her statement. "This is true? Was I never to know? Did you give no thought to telling me of my own child?"

She sat up and reached fr her blanket, then pulled it around her shoulders like an armor against the memories.

"There was no reason to tell you."

"No reason? It was my son!" His voice echoed off the rock of the small cave. "And if he'd lived, you would have kept that from me as well?"

She didn't answer. She'd made her decision almost two

years ago, and now there was nothing left but to live with it. At least she didn't need to live the the secret any longer. She'd told him, so the worst was over. She could survive Eric's rejection of her again. She'd already survived it once before.

His back to her, he stood at the entrance of the cave for several minutes. When he returned to the fire to lay out his bedding, he placed it as far away from her as he could.

Jeanne lay down again, willing a sleep that wouldn't come. She should have known better than to have allowed herself to believe even for a moment that he could ever be hers again. Happiness was not her destiny.

After a long time, Eric spoke once more. "There is no chance the babe belonged to Eymer?" His voice sounded hollow in the dark.

"None at all," she answered truthfully.

"And he was aware of that as well?"

"He was."

Eric asked no more questions and she offered no more information. All that had happened, like Eric's love for her, was in the past. Perhaps she'd at last reached a point where she could begin to work on letting go of the past to focus on her future.

CHAPTER 8

*L*etting go of the past was easier said than done when you were forced to spend your days with your arms fastened around the broad chest that had been the best part of that past.

Jeanne straightened her back, trying to put even an inch of distance between herself and Eric, a difficult task when sharing the back of a horse.

The one thing she could be thankful for was that they had left the snow behind them hours ago as they'd come down from the mountains.

"Do you see that haze on the horizon?" Eric lifted an arm to point ahead of them. "Unless I miss my guess, that's where we're headed."

Jeanne stretched to see over his shoulder. "Will we make it there before nightfall?"

"We will," he confirmed, as tight-lipped as he had been all day.

After what had passed between them last night, he'd shut himself off as completely as if they were hundreds of miles apart.

Thank the saints they were so near to their destination. She could imagine no better way to end this awful day than by fulfilling her pledge. With her goal so close, Eric's refusal to talk to her couldn't matter. Nothing mattered now except the small bundle she carried in her pack.

Another half hour of riding and the sea stretched out before them, a ribbon of bright blue, separated from them only by a strip of sandy beach at the edge of the rugged rocks they traversed.

Once they'd crossed onto the sand, Eric dismounted and lifted Jeanne down.

She gathered stones to build a small fire pit close to the water, while Eric gathered bits of driftwood and brought them to the pit.

When the tinder caught and a few small flames licked up around the wood, Jeanne kneeled by the fire and pulled the small boat from her pack. With shaking hands, she removed all the bandages and set the little sail in place. Then she adjusted the pillow in the hollow on the deck before dipping into the pack again for the little bag containing Eymer's tooth. Gently, she placed the tooth on the herb-laced pillow and started toward the water's edge.

"Wait." Eric stood next to her, a bundle of dried weeds clutched in his hand. "I need the truth from you once more, Jeanne. You say that Eymer knew the babe was mine. Did he know before you wed or after?"

The past was the past, she reminded herself, doing her best to steel her heart. She no longer had any need for secrets.

"Before," she answered, meeting Eric's gaze. "It was the reason he offered himself in marriage. To give our son a name. To give our son a father who wanted him."

"And the two of you kept this from me."

Jeanne shrugged, sighing. "Eymer counseled for yer being told the truth, but I would not agree to it."

"Why?" A suspicious shine filled Eric's eyes and he dipped his head, blinking rapidly. "Why would you withhold knowledge of my own son from me?"

"If you had wanted me and a family, you would have said so when I asked ye that we wed. You said no. I'd never hold a child over yer head to force you into something you did not want. My mother did that, and my father resented her to his dying day. He resented me, too. I'd no' have a child of mine spend his days believing himself to be the cause of his parents' misery."

Again he met her gaze. "And you feared I would turn into yer father."

Jeanne nodded her agreement.

Eric scrubbed his free hand over his face and stared out over the water. "So this is the debt you feel you owe Eymer. To repay him for his being willing to raise our son as his own."

"Yes," she whispered, turning toward the water with the little craft clutched to her breast. "Because he willingly offered up his freedom to raise my child. Because he was unendingly kind and courteous toward me. Because this was the only thing he ever asked of me in return."

"Here." Eric handed over the bundle of weeds, taking the boat with his other hand. "Use that to set fire to the ship's sail. I'll place him into the water for his journey."

She lowered the weeds to the flames. They crackled as they caught fire and she touched them to the sail. Flames licked up the fabric while Eric bent to set the little craft on its way.

In a loud, clear voice, Jeanne said, "May the mighty Thor grant you strength and courage. May he guide you on yer way. Ad may he open the doors to Valhalla to welcome you inside."

"Godspeed, Eymer Horvesson," Eric called from her side as the little craft wobbled away from the shore.

In the distance, thunder echoed, sending a shiver down Jeanne's neck. The last thing they needed on this cold night would be rain.

Dusk surrounded them as the sun seemed to float in the water on the distant horizon, casting a path of gold across the breaking waves. Together they waited, watching the fiery little vessel pitching bravely away from the shoreline, straight down the golden path as if it were being steered in that direction.

"Do you suppose his Viking gods listened to our pleas?" Eric asked.

"Eymer claimed that Thor would always come to yer aid if yer prayer was sincere." She hoped he had been right. No one deserved to be where they wanted in the afterlife more than Eymer.

They continued to watch as the sun sank below the horizon, watched until the tiny, fiery dot disappeared into the dark.

"Yer repair certainly did the job. I never thought that wee boat would said on so long." Even before the accident, she'd feared it would sink right away.

"Nor did I. Come on." Eric captured her hand and pulled her from the water's edge. "We'll camp just beyond the rocks where the grasses have taken room. We should be safe enough there."

Safe from the tide, perhaps, but the barren landscape gave no protection at all from the icy winds that now swept in from the sea.

Again they worked through building a small fire, aided only by the light of the rising moon.

When their task was finished, Jeanne sat beside the fire and wrapped her blanket around her shoulders. Eric dropped down close to her side, spreading his blanket and fur around both of them.

She snuggled gratefully under his arm, feeling as if she could easily believe herself to have been transported back to a time and place before her life had taken such a drastic turn. Back to a time and place where she still believed she would spend her life with the man seated next to her.

Staring up at the star-speckled sky, she felt a sense of peace settle over her. She'd carried out the promise she'd made and now she could get on with her life. She felt free.

And cold and hungry.

Eric's stomach rumbled, and hers echoed its response.

"I've heard tales of special men who take fish from the sea, guided only by the light of the moon," she said.

"I've heard such tales as well," Eric acknowledged, tightening is arm around her. "Unfortunately for us, I'm no one of those special men. And with that mist rolling in over te waters, I doubt even Eymer's Thor could find fish on this night."

As Eric said, it looked as though a cloud had descended upon the water's surface, and not even moonlight penetrated beyond the mist.

Jeanne laid her head against his chest, willing her stomach to silence. It had been so long since she'd eaten that even Eric's lumpy, tasteless porridge from last night sounded good right now. She was so hungry, in fact, she could swear she smelled food on the breeze.

"Close yer eyes and try to rest," he advised. "At first light I'll find something to fill our bellies; then we'll return home."

Home had such a nice ring to it.

Her eyelids were heavy, but they refused to stay shut. Tipping her head back a little she stared up at the moon, following its light down toward the black waters where the cloudy mist had begun to lift. The moon's light cut a path across the waves and up onto the sandy shore.

Its trail seemed to lead directly from the water to the place where they rested. The shining pathway glistened and beckoned, like a well-worn road to market, regularly traveled by masses of people. People like the one heading in their direction right now.

With a start, she jerked upright, unsettling the covers from her shoulders.

Next to her, Eric came instantly alert. "What is it?"

She'd thought she was dreaming, but that wasn't the case.

"There." She pointed toward the sea, toward the man who headed in their direction.

"Someone's out there."

* * *

ERIC JUMPED to his feet and drew his sword. With no place to hide, they were at a disadvantage. He reached down and clasped Jeanne's hand, pulling her to her feet.

"Should the need arise, mount up and ride as hard as you can. Doona you slow and doona you look back."

"And leave you here alone? Oh, I don't think so. Besides, He's likely no threat, out here on the shore alone as he is. I'd guess it's only our fire that draws him to us."

Indeed, their fire gave them away like an accusing finger pointing to their location. Having a fire when they were already so exposed had been a tactical error, but he'd had no choice. Either he built the fire or he risked Jeanne succumbing to the cold.

"Whether or no," he said, keeping his voice low and in control as he put his body in between Jeanne and the approaching man. "If I give you the word, yer to mount up and ride. I'll no' accept any argument on this point."

She shrugged in that annoying way she had when she disagreed with him, but he hadn't time for further discussion. As the stranger drew closer, Eric's concern grew He was a big man—far bigger than most—carrying something large over his shoulder.

"Oho, travelers!" the stranger called as soon as he was close enough. It's good to find you out here in the wilderness."

"Keep yer distance," Eric called back, holding his sword in front of him. "We've nothing here for you. No' even any food, so yer best off to just keep moving."

"We have a fire, though," Jeanne piped in. "We'll gladly share that."

"Dammit, woman!" he hissed. "Where's yer good sense?"

The man kept coming, his booming laugh echoing around them. "Then it's an excellent thing that I've found you, because I've food aplenty to share. And a much better campsite than yer own, too."When he reached them, Eric could see that the man carried a bag on his back, and from the smell, it was likely fish he had inside.

"Come on," the big man urged, kicking dirt up on their fire. "It's not far from here, but it is well sheltered from the winds."

"No, thank you. You be on yer way. We'll stay where we are."

"Eric!" Jeanne tugged at his sleeve. "Think about what you say."

He cast a look in her direction but did not speak.

"Don't be foolish, warrior. Few are given a second chance."

In the instant Eric had turned his head toward, the big man had gotten within an arm's length of him.

"You need food and I've a stew on to boil. Follow along with me and once you've eaten, if it pleases you still, you're welcome to take your leave of me."

"I did smell food," Jeanne murmured, starting off after the man as he kept walking. "It wasn't my imagination."

How was he to protect a woman such as this? He grabbed her arm, pulling her back to his side.

"Have you forgotten the lesson of Dobbie Caskie so soon? Had we left him on the rub as I wanted, we'd have food of our own right now."

Jeanne lifted her palm to his cheek, a stroke so soft he wondered for an instant if he'd imagined her touch. Then she pulled away from him.

"I willna spend my days distrusting everyone. You can stay here if you, like, Eric, but I'm going with him."

By all that was holy, Jeanne would be the death of him yet.

CHAPTER 9

"I've never seen wee bowls such as these." Jeanne scooped her bread into the best broth she'd ever tasted, serving in a small rounded bowl carved from wood. "This tastes wonderful."

The big man laughed and handed a bowl to Eric, who hovered at her side, still on his feet.

"Here. Fill your belly with this. The fish will be done soon. And we need something to drink, as well."

He pulled out three wooden cups and filled them from a large flask lying at hi side.

Jeanne accepted hers and took a sip. It reminded her of the honey wine they made at home, only sweeter and thicker on the tongue, with a sharp bite as she swallowed.

"Mead?" Eric asked, sniffing the cup he'd accepted.

"The finest you'll ever taste, warrior" the man assured.

"Eric," Jeanne corrected around another bite. "His name is Eric MacNichol and I am Jeanne MacGhie Horvesson of Castle MacGahan."

She could hardly believe they hadn't yet exchanged names. Proof of how intoxicating the food was.

"So you are," the big man said, dipping his bowl into the bubbling pot before looking up at them with a big smile. "And you may call me Halldor O'Donar."

Jeanne returned the smile as she scooped up more of the delicious, salty broth. She liked the big man. Though she should have been intimidated by his size—he stood at least a head taller than Eric—his easy manner and ready laughter gave her comfort.

"What sets you on the road so far from home, O'Donar?" Eric asked.

"A debt of honor," the big man answered without pause, his expression turning serious. "Keeping a promise to a friend."

"Us as well." The similarity only reinforced the bond Jeanne felt with Halldor. "Though ours is now fulfilled and we begin our journey on the morrow to return home."

"Indeed" Halldor rotated the stokes holding the fish over the fire. "I am but at the beginning of my journey. My friend has asked me to watch over his son. The lad is in dire near of guidance, as he is only at the beginning of his own dangerous path."

"Which direction do you travel from here?"

The tone of Eric's question made Jeanne think more of an interrogation than a visit with friends. It would seem that Eric didn't feel the same level of comfort with their new friend as she did.

"North," Halldor answered, his face breaking once again into a smile. "I believe our fish is done, from the smell of it. And where are my manners?" He stood and refilled their cups before taking the fish from the fire and passing a stake to each of them.

Eric finally sat down next to her.

The salty broth, though delicious, was stoking a mighty

thirst. She drained the contents of her cup and held it out for ore at almost the same moment Eric did.

"I'll admit that I was wrong about Dobbie," she said, by way of offering an olive branch. "But Halldor is altogether different. Surely you can feel that as well as I do."

Eric arched an eyebrow and tipped back his cup.

"Who is this Dobbie?" Halldor asked.

We met Dobbie Caskie on the side of the road as we traveled," Eric said. He claimed to be headed to his mother's people, the MacCabes, on the Isle of Skye. Jeanne here felt sorry for him and insisted that we invite him to travel with us and share what food we brought along."

He was quite young to be traveling alone and he looked so very hungry." Jeanne shook her head. "My heart went out to the poor lad."

"I would expect nothing less of you, my lady," Halldor offered gallantly. "So you shared your food with the boy."

"And the next morning," Eric continued, " this 'poor' lad of hers stole one of our horses and most of our food."

"Ah, I see. Dobbie Caskie of Skye, is it? I'll remember that name." Halldor nodded thoughtfully. "So it is for this reason that you were reluctant to accept my offer of hospitality. For many, trust doesn't come easily."

Eric looked in Jeanne's direction. "And some are much too trusting for their own good."

"Those whose hearts are open and accepting, perhaps," Halldor agreed. "But as you can see, I've food aplenty and two horses that travel with me, so you've naught to fear in this meeting."

Jeanne nodded vigorously, setting her world to spinning around her. That mead of Halldor's had quite the kick.

"I have to sleep" she said, surprised that she'd voiced the thought aloud.

"We all have a long road to travel on the morrow. You two

take your rest; I'll clean up here. No." Halldor held up a hand to stop Eric's protest. "See to your lady this night. Only a food would turn down a second chance when it's been given as a gift."

Eric spread her blanket close to the fire, and she lay down, pulling the covers up over her shoulders.

"That's the second time you've made reference to a second chance," Eric noted, his words sounding heavy and slurred. "Am I missing something yer trying to tell me?"

Halldor's laugh boomed before he answered. "Only that by the sun's rise we'll part ways, and who can know how long before we meet again?"

"*If* we'll meet again," Eric corrected, lying down next to Jeanne.

"Oh, my warrior friend, I feel sure our paths will cross again."

Jeanne sighed and snuggled back against Eric's warm body. His arm draped over her, possessively pulling her closer to him, and she had to force herself not to giggle with pleasure as his breathing turned to soft snores.

Thanks to their new friend, her stomach was full and her heart was light. This was one of the best nights she could remember in a long, long time.

CHAPTER 10

a tickling to Jeanne's nose awoke her. She lay still, hoping the irritation would disappear in no hurry to move from the warm comfort of her nest of blankets.

It was not to be. As regularly as a heartbeat, something soft flitted across her nose and back again.

She lifted a hand to discover the fur under which she slept was the culprit, blown back and forth by the slow, steady breathing of her sleeping companion.

Her sleeping companion! A trill of excitement prickled deep inside, adding to her warmth.

Cracking her eyes open only the bares slit, she discovered it was still night and, from the looks of the stars overhead, it would be a good long while before the sun made an appearance for the day. Much too early for her to move from this wonderful spot.

She shifted a bit under the big arm draped across her, and turned her face toward Eric. Her nose nestled against the base of his throat and she breathed in his essence.

How many times had she lain like this, curled into his

embrace, sheltered in his arms, awaiting the break of morning when they'd both have to return to their real lives, pretending their night together had never happened?

Eymer had been right all along.

No matter how she might fight the truth of it, she loved Eric. She had always loved him. Would always love him. She knew that now. Admitted it to herself. Her feelings for him were so much a part of her that there was no way she could separate them out and pack them away.

Perhaps this had been Eymer's purpose in insisting that Eric accompany her. Even from beyond the grave, her husband was determined to prove that he knew best.

Slowly, she moved her hand up to lay it over Eric's heart. Beneath her fingers a ragged, racing tattoo beat in his chest.

She looked up to find him watching her.

"How long has it been since I last told you how beautiful you are when you first awake?" he asked softly.

"Too long," she returned, stretching up to meet the kiss he offered.

If only it could stay like this. If only real life didn't dawn with the rising of the sun and turn them back into the enemies they'd become.

His lips were warm and tender against hers his tongue insistent in its demands as he rolled her to her back beneath him. His fingers met the challenge of her laces as skillfully as a master while she fumbled with his shirt like some inexperienced novice.

Her sift slipped from first one shoulder and then the other and his mouth covered her eager breast as her heart pounded in her chest until she thought It might break free of her ribs.

Her body thrummed with a sensitivity born from having waited so very long for this moment.

His touch was better than the finest liquid she'd ever drunk. Better than the best food she'd ever eaten, even at her hungriest. Even last night.

"By the saints," she gasped, remembering that they weren't along. "O'Donar!" she hissed.

Eric stilled. A low, frustrated growl rolled over her skin and a moment later, his head emerged from under the covers, his gaze locking with hers.

"Bollocks," he muttered under his breath.

She bit her bottom lip to stifle the irrational giggle forming in her throat and clutched the fur to her breast as she sat up.

O'Donar was nowhere to be seen. Neither him, nor his bedroll, nor the massive destrier that had been tied up next to Eric's horse.

But O'Donar's second animal remained behind, contentedly munching on the dry weeds at his feet.

"He's gone. Why would he no' stay the night in his own camp?"

"I canna say, but I'm no' really surprised," Eric answered, draping one of their blankets around her shoulders. "He as much as warned us it would be so."

"But he left his horse and one of his packs. Surely he intends to return."

She couldn't imagine leaving a valuable animal behind, but it made no sense that he'd pack up his belongings if he only intended to be away from the camp for a short time.

"A loan, perhaps?" Eric rubbed a hand over his eyes. "He did say something about seeing us again, though my memories are fair muddled after drinking that mead of his."

Her memories of the evening were slightly confused, too, as if she'd watched the events from outside their circle rather than actually participating.

"It was all very strange, do you no' agree? If no' for the horse, I could almost believe none of this happened."

"It happened, true enough." Eric tucked a loose strand of hair behind her ear, his gaze fixing upon her as his thumb lingered on her cheek. "All of it."

I suppose we should…what I mean to say is, do you think we…" Her face heated under his stroking touch and she struggled to finish her thought. "Should we prepare to leave early?"

"No," he responded, lifting his other hand to cup her face. "I think we should finish what we've begun."

"I'm no sure that's a wise path for us to take." No matter how much she might want the same thing.

"Wise or no', it's the one laid out for us to travel." He reached down for her hand, clasping it between his. "I'm slow to think a thing through, Jeanne. I take overly long to look at all sides. But I've done that now and I realize I'd be a bigger fool than I already have been if I let you slip away from me again."

He lifted her hand to his lips to place a kiss upon her palm. "None of what's passed is half so important as the love we shared. The secrets you kept are of no matter. I accept the reason you chose as you did. You did what you thought best because I was too busy trying to outwit what was to come. I see now that I canna control what the future brings. But whatever that may be, I want to meet it with you at my side, as my wife."

"Oh, Eric!" she sighed, tangling her fingers in his hair to pull his lips to meet hers.

He loved her! As he lay on his back and pulled her down on top of him, she thought her heart might burst with her happiness.

"You've yet to answer me, sweet Jeanne," he breathed into her ear. "Do you want me still? Will you take me—selfish, slow, stubborn fool that I am—as yer husband? Will you agree to spend yer life at my side?"

How could he possibly doubt her answer?

"There is nothing I want more than to spend my life with you. Yes, Eric, yes. A thousand times yes."

He rolled her to her back, swallowing her words in his kiss. With his knee, he pushed her legs apart and she welcomed him back to the spot where he belonged.

It had been such a long, long time since last he lay over her like this. She wrapped her arms around his neck and buried her nose into his strong, solid chest.

The hard, ready evidence of his desire pressed against her and she lifted her hips to meet his thrust.

"You are mine," he whispered into her ear. "Just as I am yers. Now and for all time."

He filled her, thrust after thrust, her need for him growing until the muscles in her body seized, tightening and releasing in happy little spasms that left her gasping for air.

Once more he drove inside her, holding her so close that his heartbeat drummed in her ear as he found his own release.

"This is how our lives are meant to be," he said tenderly, sweeping her sweat-dampened hair from her face. "We've been given a second chance, and I will grab on with both hands and never let go."

He rolled to her side and curved his body around hers, holding her close until his breathing turned slow and steady.

Lying comfortably snuggled in the arms of her love, Jeanne basked in the afterglow. She was the luckiest woman in the known world.

Lady Danielle had been correct. Eymer's sending her on this quest with Eric *had* been a gift.

Here life lay spread before her, her dreams waiting to be

fulfilled. Eymer had given her an opportunity for a bright future, filled with all the possibilities she could ever desire.

Thank you, Eymer Horvesson.

Snuggling back against the man she loved with all her heart, she hoped that wherever Eymer's spirit was, he heard and knew how much she would always treasure her warrior's last gift.

OTHER BOOKS BY MELISSA MAYHUE:

~ Magic of Time Series ~

1 - All the Time You Need

2 - Anywhere In Time

3 - Time to Spare (Coming 2019)

~Chance, Colorado Series~

(Contemporary Romance)

1 - Take a Chance

2 - Second Chance at Love (Coming 2019)

~ Daughters of the Glen Series ~

1 - Thirty Nights with a Highland Husband

2 - Highland Guardian

3 - Soul of a Highlander

4 - A Highlander of Her Own

5 - A Highlander's Destiny

6 - A Highlander's Homecoming

7 - Healing the Highlander

8 - Highlander's Curse

~ Warriors Series ~

1 - Warrior's Redemption

2 - Warrior's Last Gift (Novella)

3 - Warrior Reborn

4 - Warrior Untamed

ABOUT THE AUTHOR

MELISSA MAYHUE, married and the mother of three sons, lives at the foot of the Rockies in beautiful Northern Colorado with her family and one very spoiled Boston Terrier. In addition to writing *The Magic of Time* Series, she has also written two additional related paranormal historical series, *The Daughters of the Glen* Series and *The Warriors* series. She is also writing *The Chance, Colorado* Series, a contemporary feel good romances set in a small mountain town.

Want to be notified when the next book is due out? Sign up for Melissa's New Release Newsletter.

If you enjoyed this book, please consider leaving a review at your favorite online retailer or at Goodreads to help other readers find it.

Get social! Connect with Melissa online:

Reader Group:
www.facebook.com/groups/Magic.of.Time
Website:
https://www.melissamayhue.com
email:
melissa@melissamayhue.com

Made in the USA
Monee, IL
20 November 2019